EPISODE I

I Am a Queen

by Amidala

as told to Alice Alfonsi
Interior design by Iain Morris

A Random House *Star Wars*® Storybook

Random House
New York

 Published in the United States by Random House, Inc., New York, and simultaneously in Canada by Random House of Canada Limited, Toronto. Used under authorization. First Random House printing, March 2000.

www.randomhouse.com/kids
www.starwars.com

Library of Congress Catalog Card Number: 99-67460
ISBN: 0-375-80523-0
Printed in the United States of America
10 9 8 7 6 5 4 3 2 1

My name is Amidala.

I am a Queen.

Naboo

The world I rule is called Naboo.

It is a peaceful planet
of green fields, swampy lakes,
and sparkling seas.

Against the blackness of space,
Naboo shimmers blue.

This is how it looks
from a starship.

Farm Girl to Princess

I was not always Queen of Naboo.
I grew up as a simple farm girl
in a tiny mountain village.

I was happy working the land
with my mother and father.

**But I was born with
the heart of a leader.**

So I studied hard and waited
for a chance to lead my people.

When I turned twelve,
I got my chance.

I was elected **Princess of Theed** and governed
a whole city.

Theed

Theed is a rich city of grand buildings, stone archways, and steep waterfalls.

It is my favorite city on Naboo.

As the capital city, Theed is also the place where Naboo's leaders work and live.

Princess to Queen

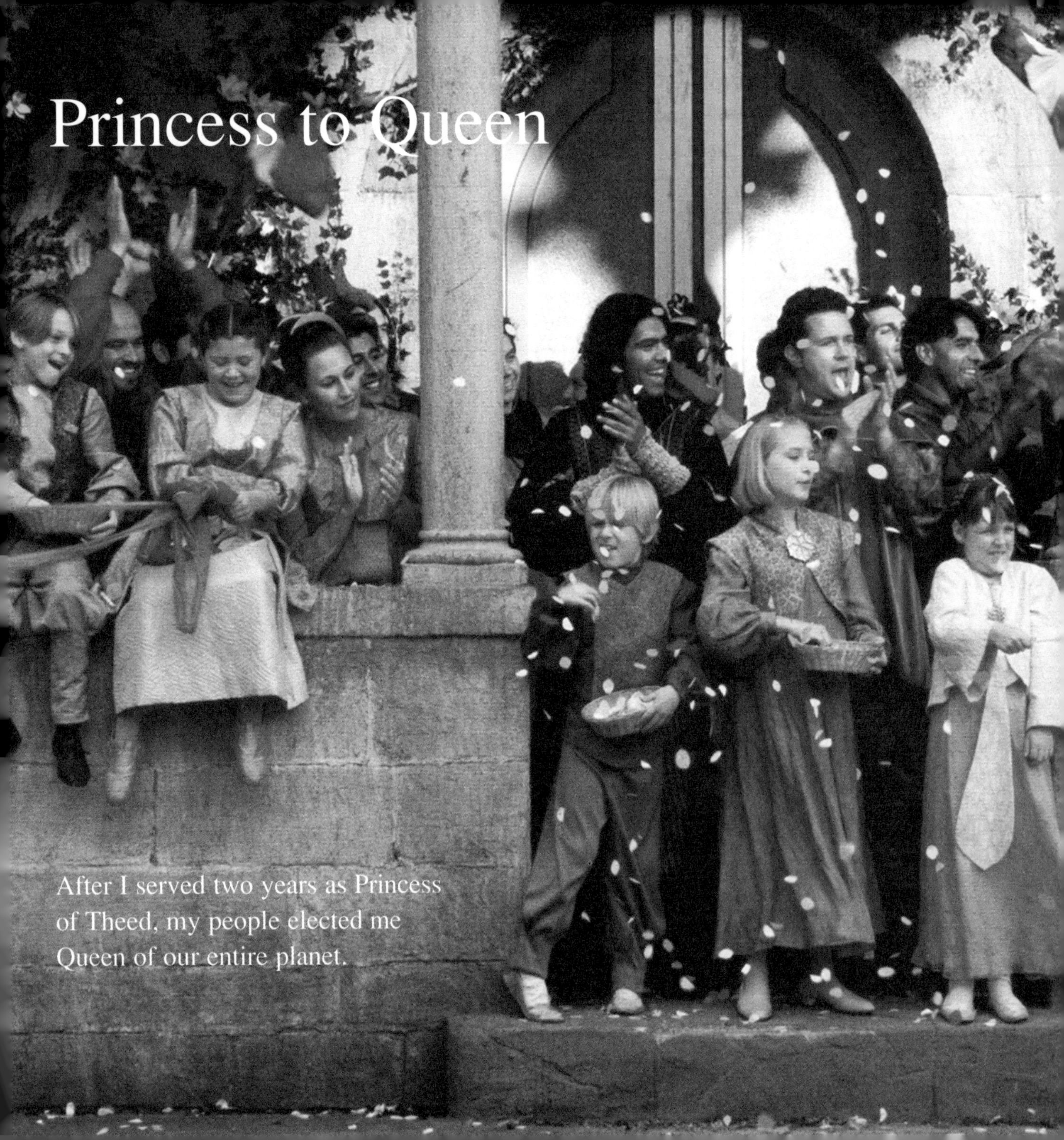

After I served two years as Princess of Theed, my people elected me Queen of our entire planet.

The people of Naboo
are as important to me
as my own family.

I will do anything
to help them live in
peace and **harmony**.

Because I am only fourteen,
a few say I am too young to be Queen.

I have always believed it is **wisdom**,
not age, that truly matters.

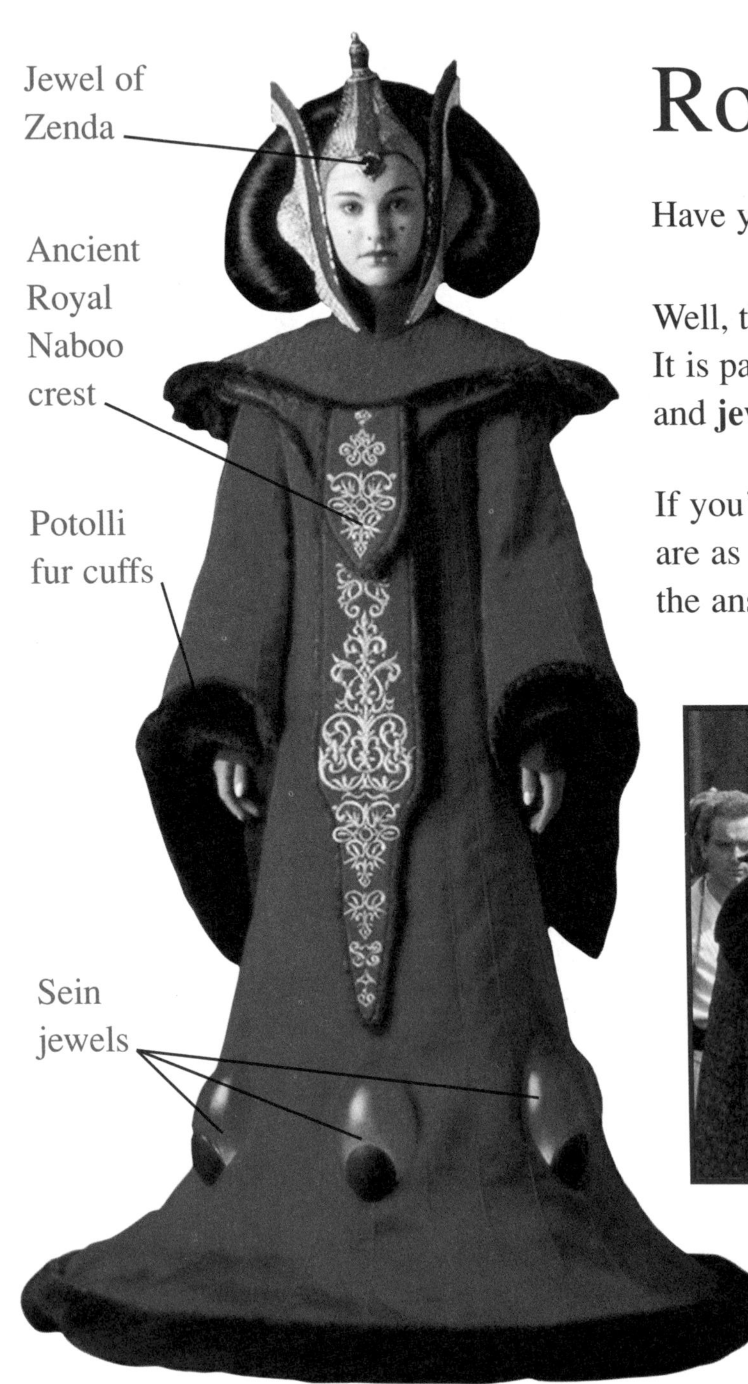

Royal Wardrobe

Have you ever heard of **"dressing the part"**?

Well, that's what I must do as Queen.
It is part of my job to wear the **royal clothing** and **jewels** of Naboo.

If you're wondering whether my fine costumes are as difficult to wear as they look, the answer is **yes!**

Still, I am happy to wear them.

My gowns remind my people of both the importance of my role and our planet's history.

Special occasions call for special gowns. This is the gown I wear for parades and celebrations.

The cape of this gown was made to look like the petals of a rare Naboo flower.

My white-and-red makeup is an ancient Naboo custom. The red mark on my lips is called the **"Scar of Remembrance."**

I wear it to remember those who gave their lives for Naboo's peace.

Galactic Senate

The most regal
of all my gowns
is this one.

I wear it whenever
I speak to the
Galactic Senate.

The Senate's
members meet
in a very large
room called
the Senate
Chamber.

Here is
where they
make decisions
that affect
thousands
of planets in
the galaxy.

Naboo is
only one
of these
planets.

You may wonder if appearing before
the Galactic Senate makes me nervous.

I'll tell you a secret—it does!

But whenever I feel unsure of myself,
I remember that my people are depending on me.

My **love** for
them gives
me **strength**.

Royal Starship

Whenever I take trips to places like the Galactic Senate Chamber, I use my Royal Starship.

Inside this ship is a **beautiful** living space for me and my handmaidens.

I even have a throne room for meeting with visitors.

Here you see me speaking with two **noble** Jedi.

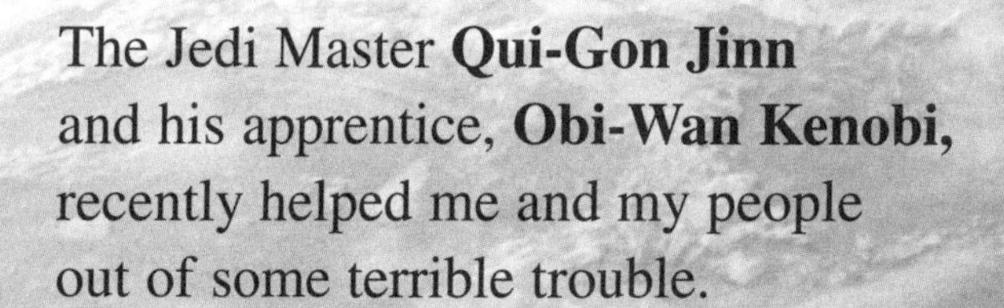

The Jedi Master **Qui-Gon Jinn** and his apprentice, **Obi-Wan Kenobi,** recently helped me and my people out of some terrible trouble.

The Trade Federation invaded Naboo and tried to imprison me.

The Jedi helped us defeat our enemies and bring peace back to Naboo.

I am happy to call the Jedi my friends!

Theed Palace

When I am not traveling in my starship, I live in the Theed Royal Palace.

It is the **grandest** building in the city of Theed, and it has many rooms for **important** meetings, dinners, and other court occasions.

Statues of famous citizens of Naboo

Throne Room

At the center
of the Theed Palace
is my throne room.

Here is where
I make decisions that
will help my people.

Here is also where I greet leaders from
other planets and meet with my advisors.

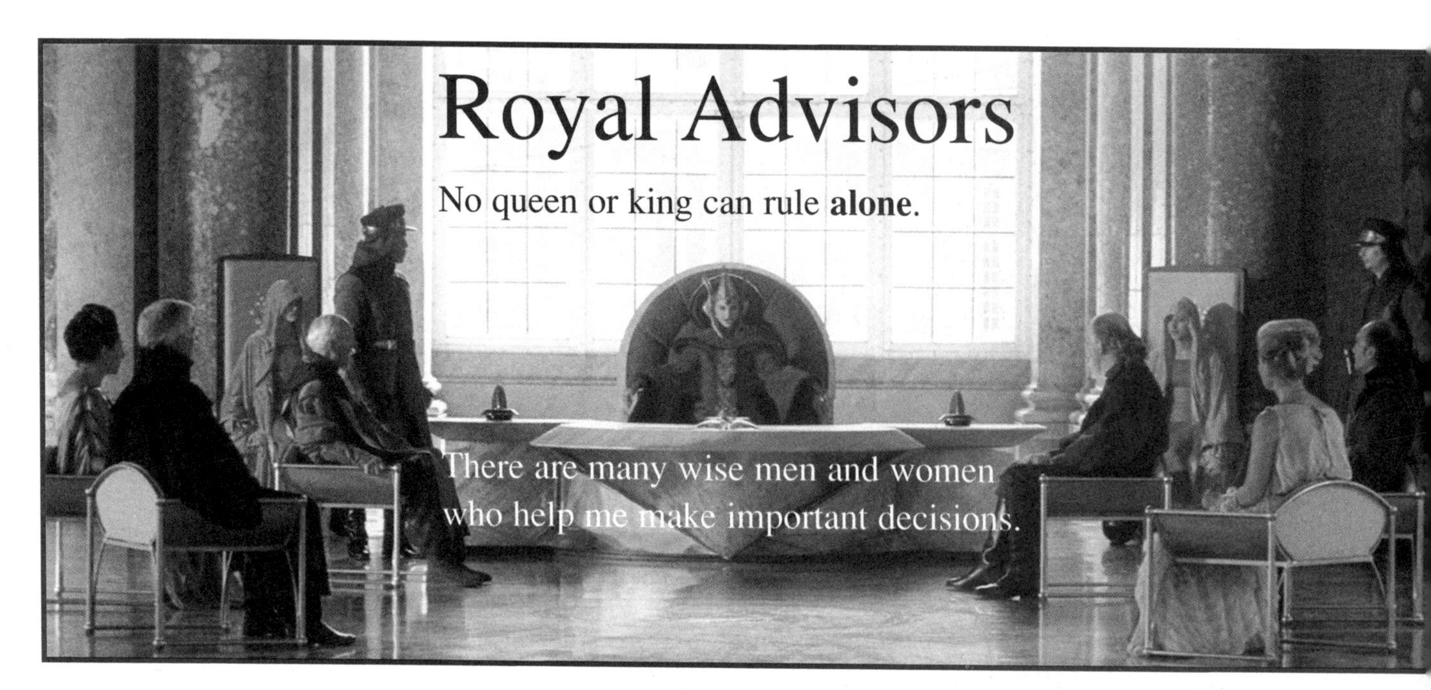

Royal Advisors

No queen or king can rule **alone**.

There are many wise men and women who help me make important decisions.

They are my **Royal Advisory Council.**

The head of the Council is **Governor Sio Bibble**.

I trust Governor Bibble and rely on his help, **especially during a crisis**.

Sio Bibble
Governor of Naboo
Lufta Shif
Education Regent
Hela Brandes
Music Advisor
Hugo Eckener
Chief Architect
Graf Zapalo
Master of Sciences

Royal Decoy

The **Queen** of Naboo always **appears** calm and serious.

But it is not always **me** under those royal robes.

When **danger** is near, I must **hide** behind a mask for my own protection.

I become **Padmé Naberrie** and pretend to be a royal handmaiden.

Look closely here and you will see that my handmaiden **Sabé** is wearing the Queen's gown.

You will also see that I am dressed as the handmaiden **Padmé**.

Sometimes I think of **Padmé** as the girl I might have been if I'd never left the village of my birth.

Though **Padmé** is just a disguise, I don't always know where she ends and **Queen Amidala** begins.

Of course, a simple farm girl would never have been trained to defend her planet!

Queen's Handmaidens

I have five handmaidens,
who help me
with my duties.

Their names are
Sabé, **Rabé,**
Yané, Saché,
and **Eirtaé**.

Each of my handmaidens
is a trained bodyguard.
In an emergency,
they all know how to protect
me and themselves.

Eirtaé has been trained in manners.

She knows the traditions of Naboo and advises me about them.

Rabé is the youngest handmaiden.

She helps with my clothes, hair, and makeup.

Royal Naboo Security Forces

Naboo's Security Forces were formed to **defend** our planet from attack.

When an off-world enemy threatens Naboo's **peace**, I look to the men and women of the Security Forces for help.

The Security Forces are made up of Security **Guards** and Security **Officers**.

Security Officer

Their head is **Captain Panaka**.

He learned much about combat by battling space pirates!

The Royal Palace Guard is the top team within the Security Forces.

It is the Palace Guard's job to **protect** the Queen and her court.

Being Queen
comes with
a price.

It can be very
difficult and
very **lonely**.

All the guards and
advisors in the
galaxy cannot do
my job for me.

So I must look inside
myself for the **wisdom**
and **strength** to guide
my people.

Only then can I be the kind
of **brave** and **noble** leader
that every Naboo citizen
is proud to call Queen.